BUZ

BUZ

RICHARD EGIELSKI

A LAURA GERINGER BOOK
AN IMPRINT OF HARPERCOLLINS PUBLISHERS

Library of Congress Cataloging-in-Publication Data
Egielski, Richard.
  Buz / by Richard Egielski.
    p.   cm.
  "A Laura Geringer book."
  Summary: When a little boy swallows a bug along with his cereal, pandemonium
breaks out as the bug searches for an escape, the boy searches for an antidote, and
Keystone Cops-like pills search for the bug.
  ISBN 0-06-023566-7. — ISBN 0-06-023567-5 (lib. bdg.)
  [1. Insects—Fiction.   2. Humorous stories.]   I. Title.
PZ7.E3215Bu   1995   94-36033
[E]—dc20   CIP
                                                                      AC

Typography by Christine Kettner
1   2   3   4   5   6   7   8   9   10
❖
First Edition

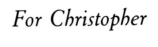

For Christopher

One morning, Buz, a bug, was eaten along with a spoonful of cornflakes. "Buzzz?" said Buz.

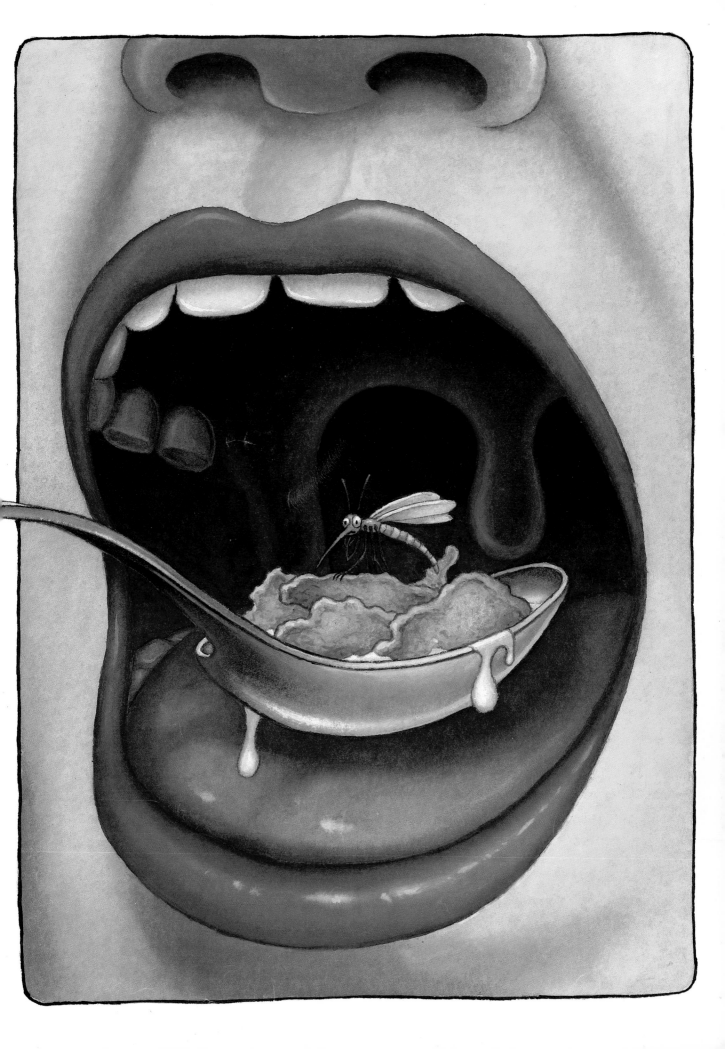

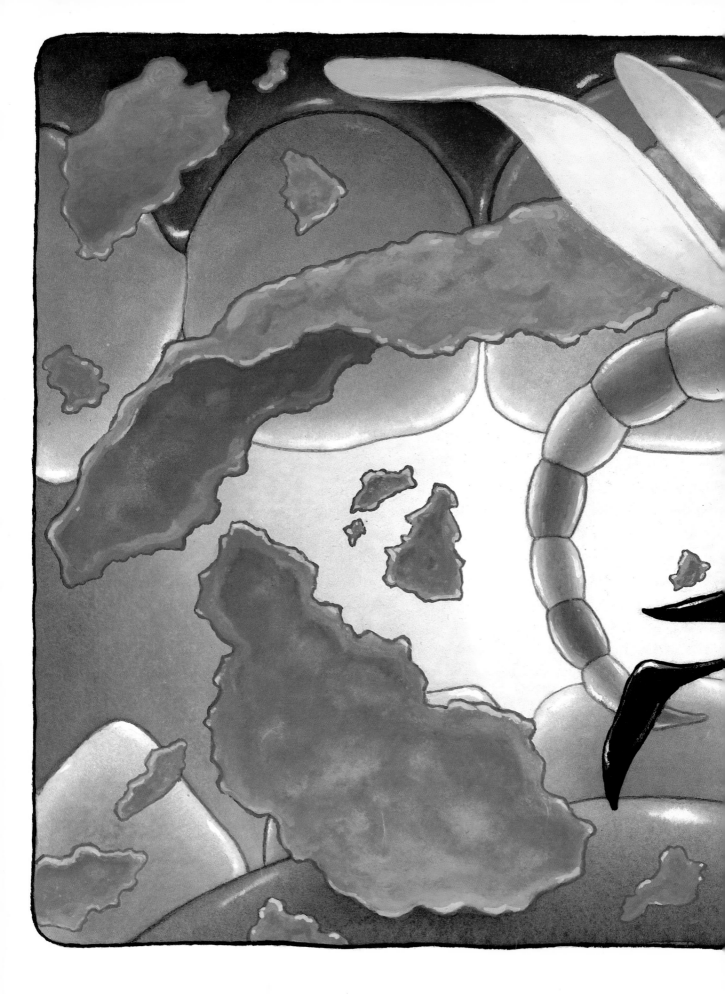

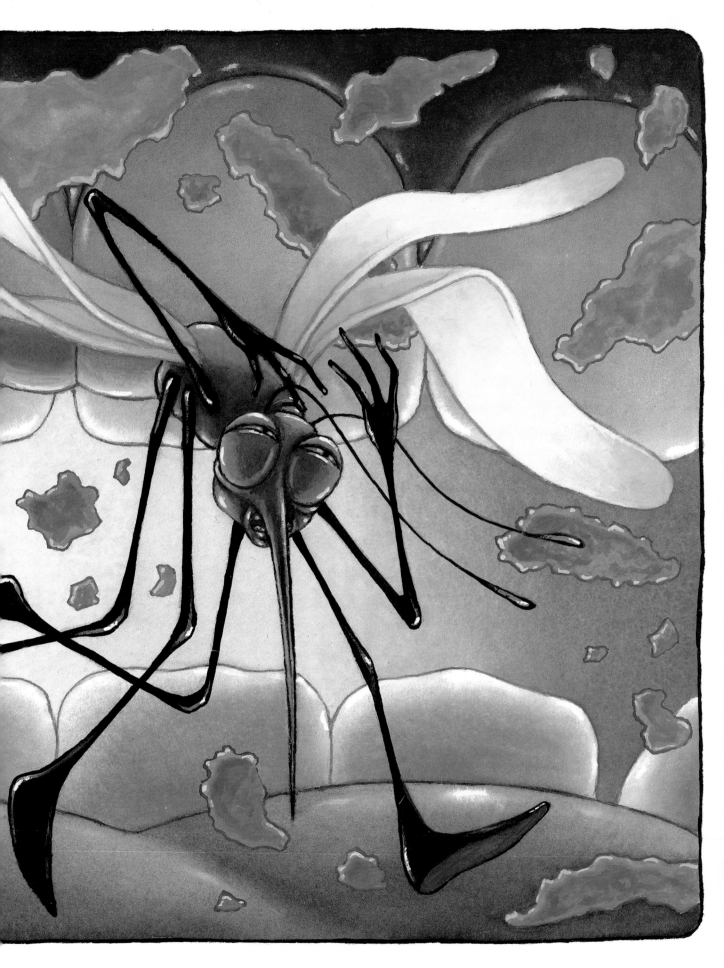

Molars mashed and flakes flew as Buz tried to escape.

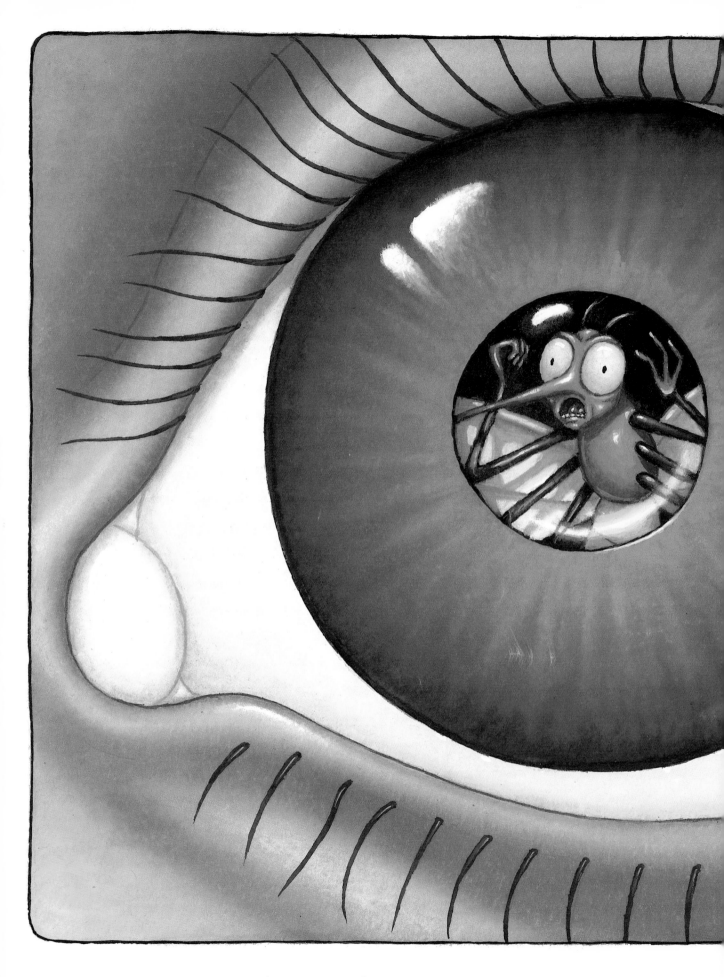

But he went the wrong way.

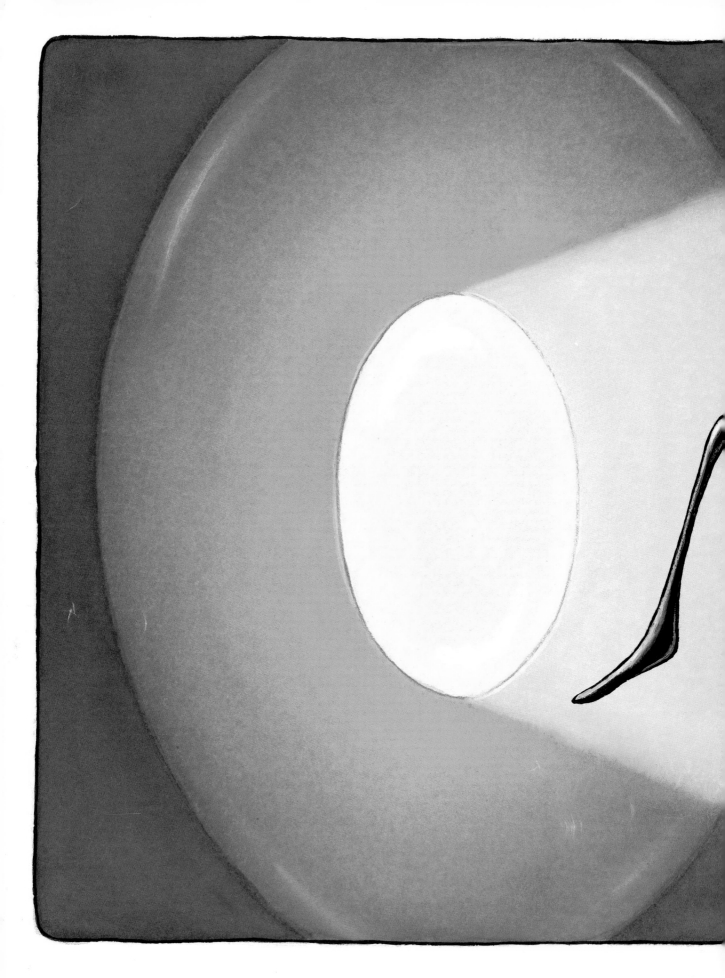

Around and around he whirled,

until suddenly a bright light flashed on.

"Tsk, tsk, tsk," said the doctor, "you caught a bug alright. I'm going to give you some pills. They'll get rid of that bug."

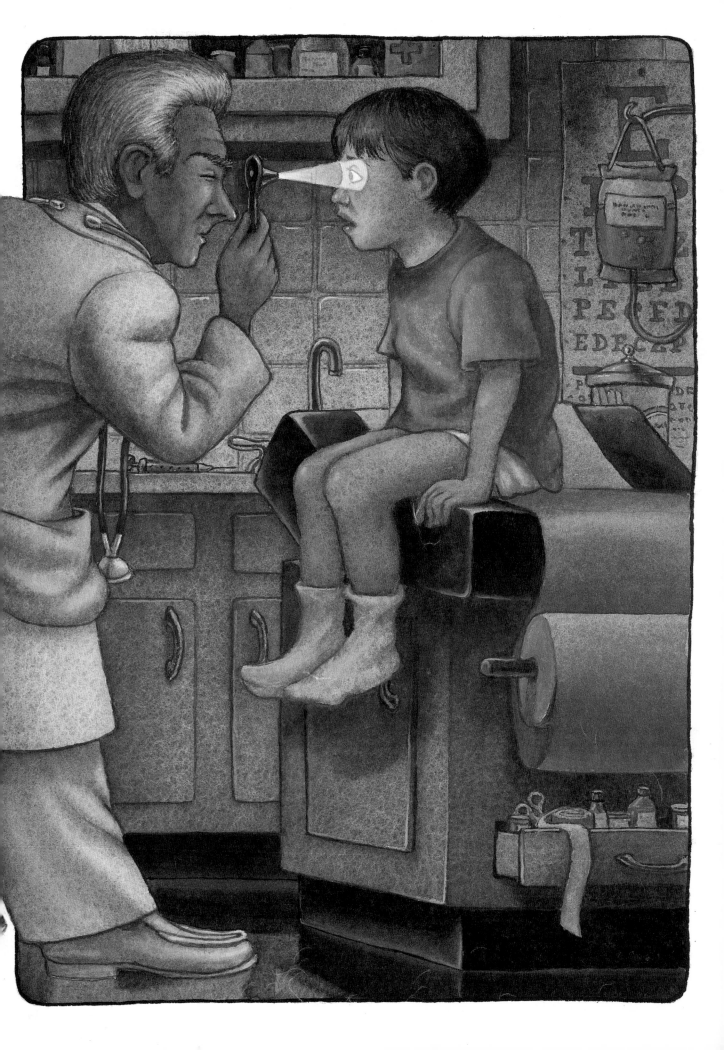

The pills went to work.

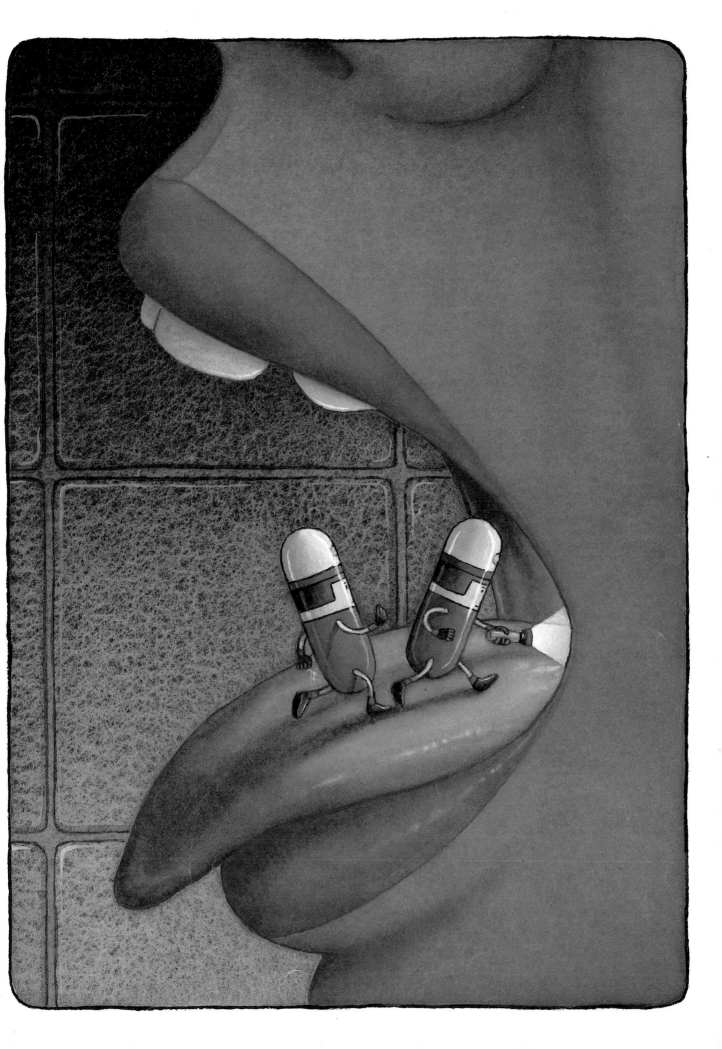

In no time they tracked Buz down.
"Hey, you with the wings! Freeze!"

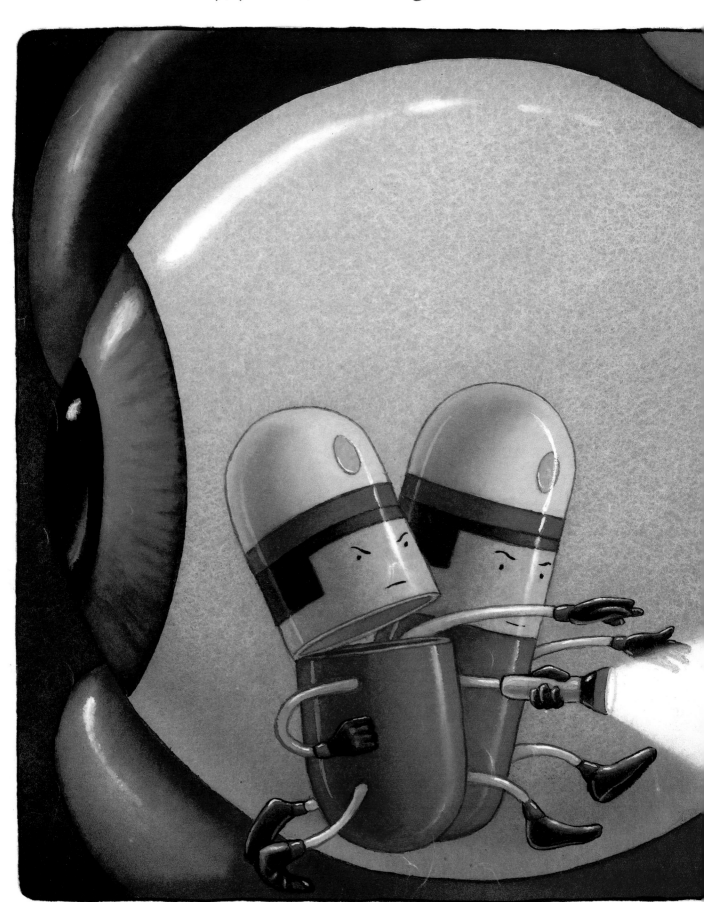

Buz took off.

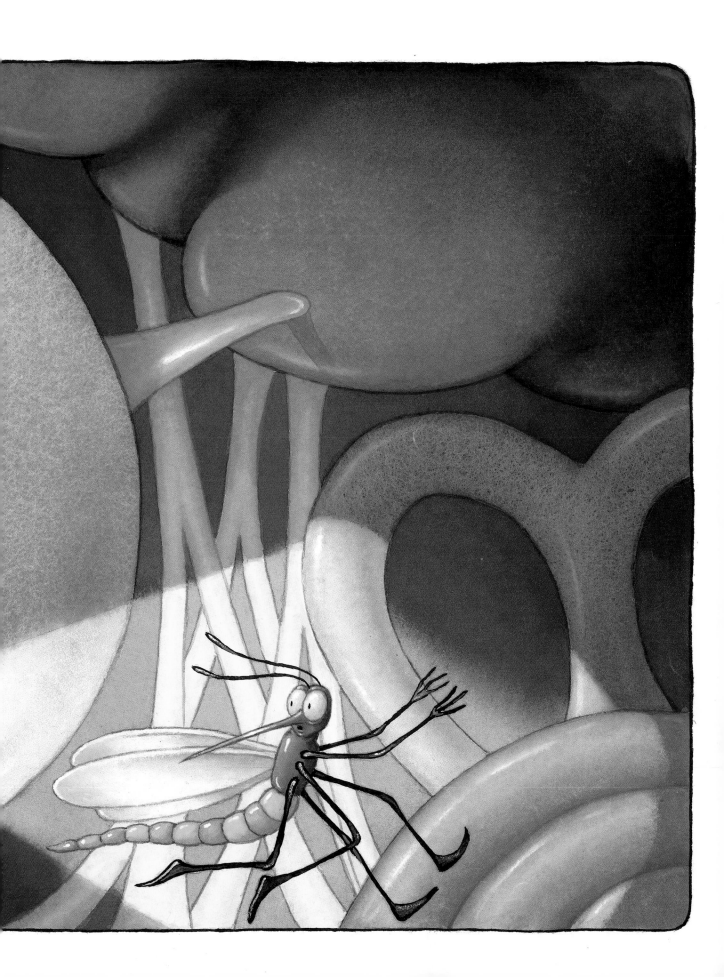

The pills searched high and low.
"See him?" said one.

"No. He got away," said the other.

Buz hid for a long time. Then, very slowly, he crept out.

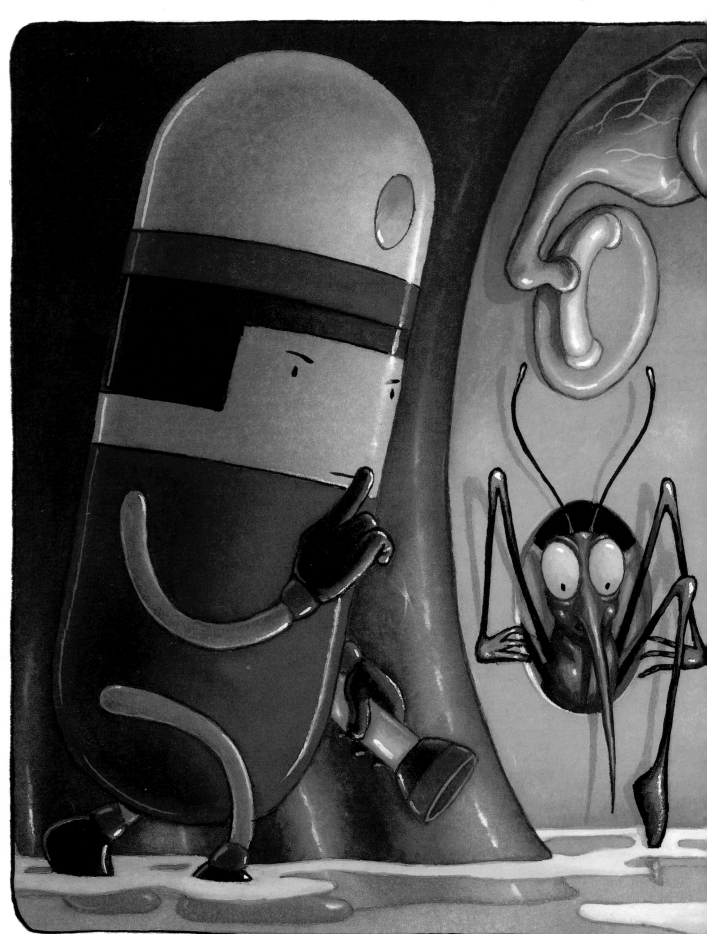

"Buzzz?" said Buz.

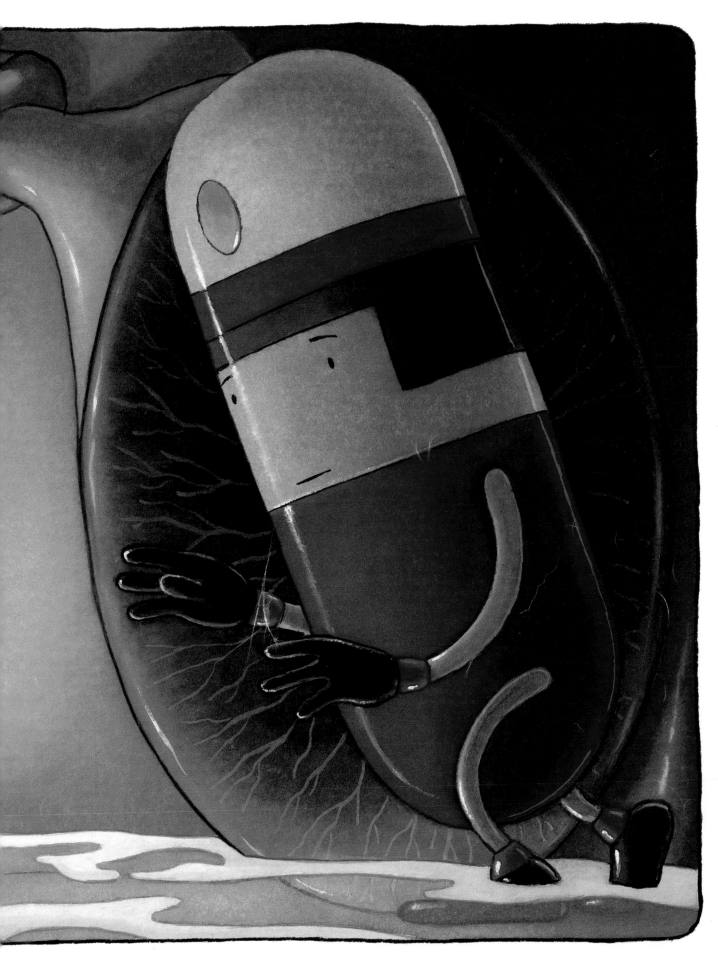

"Aha!" cried the pills.

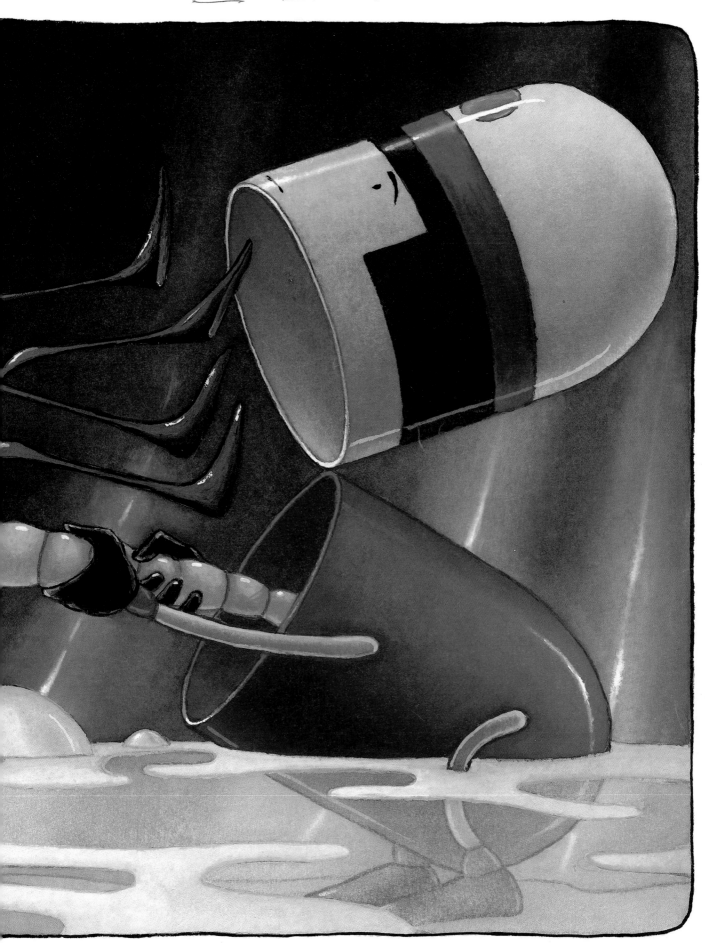

"Stop!" they gurgled.

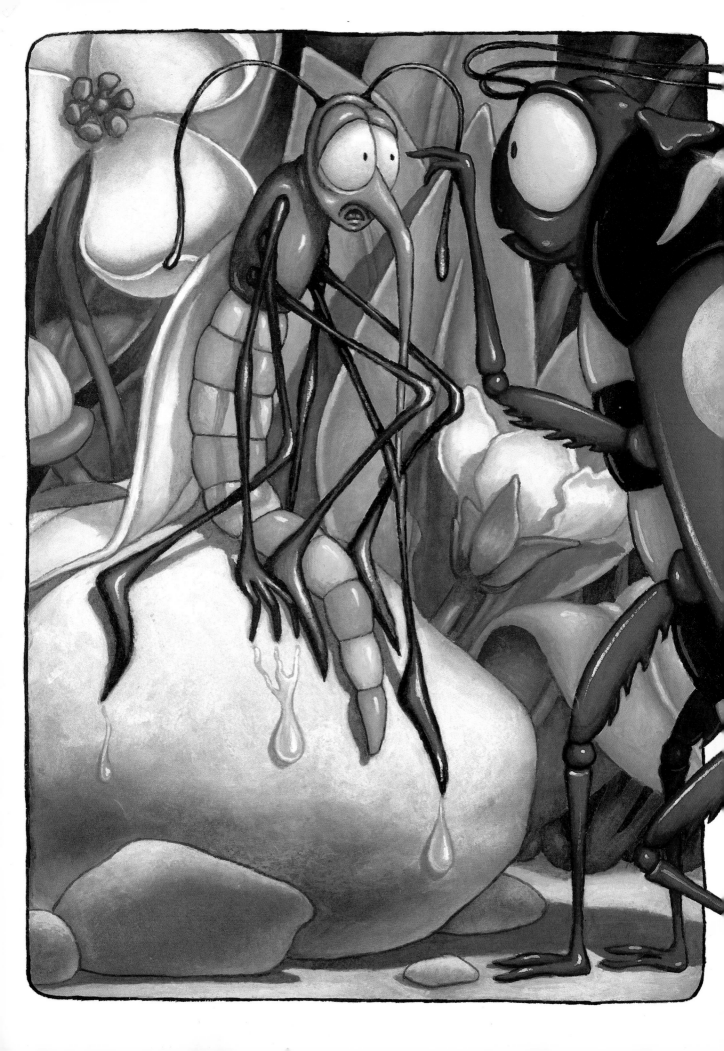

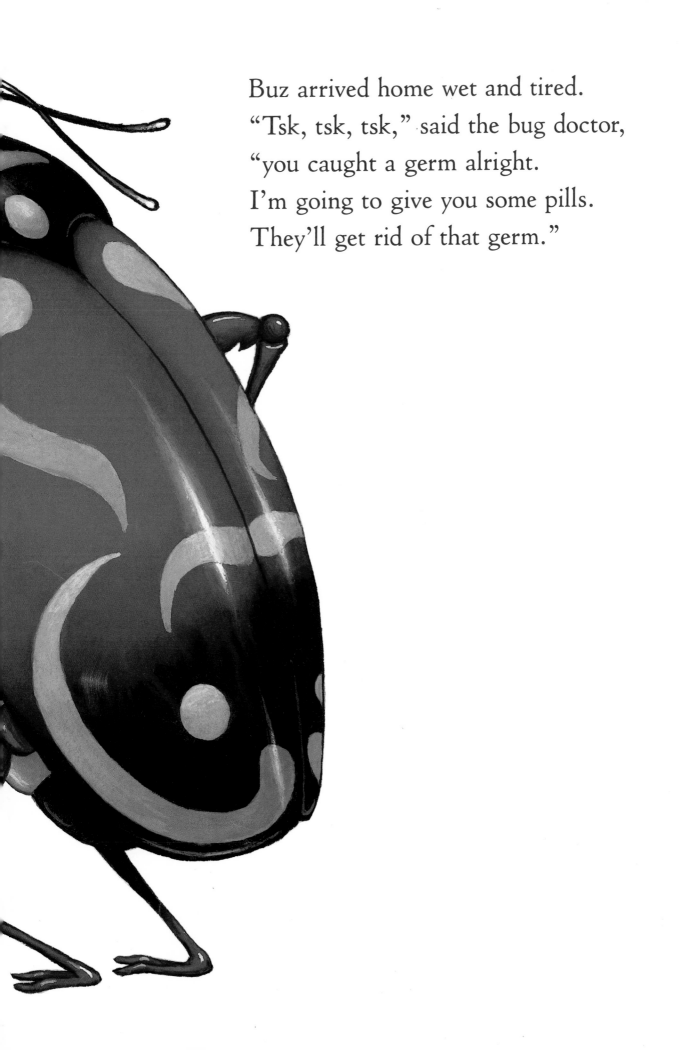

Buz arrived home wet and tired.
"Tsk, tsk, tsk," said the bug doctor,
"you caught a germ alright.
I'm going to give you some pills.
They'll get rid of that germ."

"Buzzz?" said Buz.